W9-AHE-543

The Very Bumpy Bus
Ride

Muntean, Michaela
Points:0.5 Lvl:2.8

THE VERY BUMPY BUS RIDE

To librarians, parents, and teachers:

The Very Bumpy Bus Ride is a Parents Magazine READ ALOUD Original — one title in a series of colorfully illustrated and fun-to-read stories that young readers will be sure to come back to time and time again.

Now, in this special school and library edition of *The Very Bumpy Bus Ride,* adults have an even greater opportunity to increase children's responsiveness to reading and learning — and to have fun every step of the way.

When you finish this story, check the special section at the back of the book. There you will find games, projects, things to talk about, and other educational activities designed to make reading enjoyable by giving children and adults a chance to play together, work together, and talk over the story they have just read.

For a free color catalog describing Gareth Stevens's list of high-quality books, call 1-800-341-3569 (USA) or 1-800-461-9120 (Canada).

Parents Magazine READ ALOUD Originals:

Golly Gump Swallowed a Fly
The Housekeeper's Dog
Who Put the Pepper in the Pot?
Those Terrible Toy-Breakers
The Ghost in Dobbs Diner
The Biggest Shadow in the Zoo
The Old Man and the Afternoon Cat
Septimus Bean and His Amazing Machine
Sherlock Chick's First Case
A Garden for Miss Mouse
Witches Four
Bread and Honey
Pigs in the House
Milk and Cookies
But No Elephants
No Carrots for Harry!
Snow Lion
Henry's Awful Mistake

The Fox with Cold Feet
Get Well, Clown-Arounds!
Pets I Wouldn't Pick
Sherlock Chick and the Giant
    Egg Mystery
Cats! Cats! Cats!
Henry's Important Date
Elephant Goes to School
Rabbit's New Rug
Sand Cake
Socks for Supper
The Clown-Arounds Go On Vacation
The Little Witch Sisters
The Very Bumpy Bus Ride
Henry Babysits
There's No Place Like Home
Up Goes Mr. Downs

Library of Congress Cataloging-in-Publication Data

Muntean, Michaela.
    The very bumpy bus ride / by Michaela Muntean : pictures by Bernard Wiseman.
        p. cm. — (Parents magazine read aloud original)
    Summary: The people, animals, strawberries, and cream of Rumbletown are given a bumpy ride to the county fair.
    ISBN 0-8368-0980-7
    [1. Buses—Fiction. 2. Fairs—Fiction.] I. Wiseman, Bernard, ill. II. Title. III. Series.
[PZ7.M929Ve 1993]
[E]—dc20   933-13042

This North American library edition published in 1993 by Gareth Stevens Publishing, 1555 North RiverCenter Drive, Suite 201, Milwaukee, Wisconsin 53212, USA, under an arrangement with Parents Magazine Press, New York.

Text © 1981 by Michaela Muntean. Illustrations © 1981 by Bernard Wiseman. Portions of end matter adapted from material first published in the newsletter *From Parents to Parents* by the Parents Magazine Read Aloud Book Club, © 1990 by Gruner + Jahr, USA, Publishing; other portions © 1993 by Gareth Stevens, Inc.

Printed in the United States of America

1 2 3 4 5 6 7 8 9 9 98 97 96 95 94 93

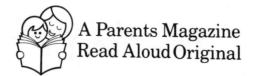

THE VERY BUMPY BUS RIDE

COUNTY FAIR

847 K

story by Michaela Muntean
pictures by B. Wiseman

Gareth Stevens Publishing • Milwaukee
Parents Magazine Press • New York

To my mother and father
—*M. M.*

For Mike and Andy
—*B.W.*

The Rumbletown Bus stopped
at Number One Bumble Street.
Mrs. Fitzwizzle climbed on board
carrying her prize strawberries
to take to the county fair.

The doors closed with a swish,
and off they went —
bumping and bouncing down Bumble Street.
"My, my," said Mrs. Fitzwizzle.
"This is a very *bumpy* bus ride."

Suddenly the bus bounced to a stop.
HONK, HONK.
The bus driver sounded his horn.
"Honk, honk, yourself,"
answered a gaggle of geese.
"Is this the bus to the county fair?"
"Yes it is," said the driver.

So the gaggle of geese waddled
onto the Rumbletown Bus.

At Number Four Bumble Street,
Mr. Flapsaddle climbed on.
He was carrying two bottles
of fresh cream to take to the fair.
"Good morning," Mr. Flapsaddle said
to a goose nearby.
"Honk, honk," the goose answered.

Then the bus started with a jerk,
and off they went —
bumping and bouncing down Bumble Street.
"My goodness!" cried Mr. Flapsaddle.
"This is a very bumpy, *noisy* bus ride!"

15

When the bus stopped again,
it was for Granny Smith's pickup truck.
"My truck won't start," Granny said.
"And my cat, Crabapple, and I have a load
of prize apples to take to the county fair."

"Don't worry," said the driver.
"We can tie your truck
to the back of the bus
which is going to the county fair."
"Good idea!" Granny said.

So they tied the truck
to the back of the bus,
and off they went —
bumping and bouncing down Bumble Street.
"Hang on to your whiskers!"
Granny called to Crabapple.

18

19

They hadn't gone far
before the bus stopped again.
"Moo-oove!" the driver called to a cow.
"Moo yourself," the cow answered.
"Is this the bus to the fair?"
"Yes it is," said the driver.
So the cow climbed on board.

The last stop was at
Number Six Bumble Street.
Billy McNilly was waiting to take
his pet goldfish, Herbert, to the fair.
Herbert could swim in perfect circles
and Billy was going to enter him
in the pet contest.

They squeezed onto the bus,
and off they went —
bumping and bouncing down Bumble Street.
"Jumping jellybeans!" cried Billy McNilly.
"This is a very bumpy, noisy, *crowded* bus ride!"

Suddenly, the bus stopped again.
But this time it did not stop for a passenger.
It did not stop for a gaggle of geese,
a cow, or a broken-down pickup truck.

It stopped for a hill.
A big, steep hill.

"Everyone out!" the bus driver called.
"We can't make it up this hill."
"But how will we get to the fair?"
Granny asked.

"I'll pull," said the cow.

"We'll push," the others said.

"And we'll honk and let everyone know
we're coming," said the geese.

27

So they huffed,
and puffed,
and pushed,
and pulled,

and honked,
and mooed,
until finally...

the Rumbletown Bus was on top of
the Bumble Street hill.
And there was the county fair
at the bottom.
"Hooray!" everyone cheered.

But before they could get back on the bus…

it started rolling down the hill all by itself!

"My *bus!*" cried the driver.

"My *strawberries!*" cried Mrs. Fitzwizzle.

"My *cream!*" cried Mr. Flapsaddle.

"My *apples!*" cried Granny Smith.

"*HERBERT!*" cried Billy McNilly.

They all ran after the Rumbletown Bus.
It was rumbling and roaring,
and jiggling and jostling,

and bumping and bouncing
faster and faster
down the Bumble Street hill.

Crash! Bang!   Clunk!   Pop!
The bus stopped right outside
the Rumbletown County Fair.

"Oh, no!" everyone cried when they saw
the strawberries and cream and apples
all over the bus.
And Herbert wasn't swimming
in perfect circles anymore.
He was hopping up and down!

The judges came out to see what had happened.
One judge wiped some strawberries off the bus.
"Mmm ... delicious strawberry jam! First prize!"
And he handed Mrs. Fitzwizzle a blue ribbon.

"This is the best whipped cream
I ever tasted!"
said another judge as she handed
Mr. Flapsaddle a blue ribbon.

Granny Smith won first prize
for her applesauce.
And Billy's fish, Herbert, won the pet prize.
After all, he was the only fish at the fair
that could hop instead of swim.

Everyone clapped and cheered.
Then they all had a wonderful time
at the Rumbletown County Fair.

And it was all because of...

the very bumpy bus ride.

Notes to Grown-ups

Major Themes

Here is a quick guide to the significant themes and concepts at work in *The Very Bumpy Bus Ride*:

- Working together: The people and animals must work together to accomplish a difficult task, pushing the bus up the hill.
- Distinguishing sounds: The animals and transportation vehicles make distinct sounds that we recognize.

Step-by-step Ideas for Reading and Talking

Here are some ideas for further give-and-take between grown-ups and children. The following topics encourage creative discussion of *The Very Bumpy Bus Ride* and invite the kind of open-ended response consistent with many contemporary approaches to reading, including Whole Language:

- The illustrations in this story include a variety of animals, such as dogs, cats, geese, sheep, cows, and many others. Your child may enjoy identifying them, naming them, and even imitating the sounds they make. This book is filled with noises and lots of fun.
- After reading this book, a discussion might lead to interesting discoveries about how foods can change. You and your child can also share the experience of making applesauce, whipped cream, or jam. You might even want to shake heavy cream into butter or mash peanuts to make peanut butter.
- Some situations don't go according to plan, although in the end they still turn out all right. Events went awry in the story, but ended happily. Can your child think of similar happenings?

Games for Learning

Games and activities can stimulate young readers and listeners alike to find out more about words, numbers, and ideas. Here are more ideas for turning learning into fun:

Tasty Treats

What a mess! Strawberries, cream, and apples all over the bus. But place those same ingredients in a blender or mash them in a bowl, and you can create a terrific treat with your child. To keep it healthy, use yogurt or milk instead of cream and sweeten with mashed banana. For variety, experiment with different fruits and leave dairy products out altogether on some concoctions. Make several kinds of blender drinks with fruits or mash them into fruit sauces and then see which one your family honors with first prize.

Variations:

Try the taste test by blindfolding your panel of judges. See if your child and the rest of the family can pass the taste test by playing "name that fruit." With a scarf tied over the contestant's eyes, give each a small bite of fruit:
1. while she or he is holding her or his nose.
2. allowing her or him to sniff it first.

Let your child discover how important a role our sense of smell plays in tasting foods and noticing differences between pears and apples, oranges and tangerines.

Give points for the number of fruits each contestant can guess correctly. The winner gets to skip out of helping clean up the kitchen!

About the Author

MICHAELA MUNTEAN was on a New York City bus one morning when she noticed a woman across the aisle with a full bag of groceries on her lap. "Every time we hit a bump or a pothole," says Ms. Muntean, "that bag would bounce on the woman's lap until finally things actually fell out and started rolling down the aisle." As Ms. Muntean helped the woman gather her things, her imagination started working. When Ms. Muntean reached home, she started writing *The Very Bumpy Bus Ride*.

Ms. Muntean, who has written many well-loved children's books, lives in New York City.

About the Artist

BERNARD WISEMAN says that the Rumbletown roads remind him of the roads in his old home town in Connecticut. "Those roads were so bumpy," he says, "that our car once broke down completely after hitting a really big bump."

Mr. Wiseman was a *New Yorker* cartoonist for many years. He left cartooning to write and illustrate children's books and has written more than thirty to date.

Mr. Wiseman now lives in Florida with his wife and children. He is happy to report that the roads are much smoother where he lives now.